To , Kenneth
Love , Carolynn & Wayne
Aug 4, 1990

ISBN 0 86163 114 5

Copyright © 1984 Award Publications Limited
Spring House, Spring Place
London NW5, England

Printed in Belgium

SLEEPYTIME tales

Written by Hayden McAllister

AWARD PUBLICATIONS – LONDON

Flying Mice

Tiny and Tubby wanted to do some hang-gliding . . . but how? Tiny mouse put his thinking cap on and came up with an idea.

Later, Tiny and Tubby mouse crept through the undergrowth near the big ponds.

"S-sh!" cried Tiny. "Don't make a sound!"

"I'm not. I never even squeaked," said Tubby.

They moved forward, whiskers twitching; and stopped.

"There it is!" said Tiny, pointing. A big sign read: 'Toodlepop Pond'. "Now we want to find the bird."

The big white bird was a stork, and it slept on the bank of the pond.

"P-sst!" said Tiny in the stork's ear. "Will you take us hang-gliding on the Big Hill please?"

"Of course," said the stork. "But how will you hang on once we're in the air?"

"We've brought our safety belts," squeaked Tiny. "I'll tie myself to your left foot, and Tubby will tie himself to your right foot."

Soon they were ready for take-off. Five minutes later they were flying high over the Big Hill.

Balloons!

It was an Autumn day and the leaves were turning brown upon the trees. In the park the children were playing. A gentle wind was blowing across the grass and songbirds were singing.

Sarah looked up into the sky and saw a golden ball drifting through the air.

"Look!" she gasped. "What is it? It's almost the colour of sunshine!"

The other children stopped playing and watched as the golden ball floated slowly higher and higher.

"It's a balloon," said one of the boys.

"Yes. But where did it come from?" asked his friend.

Then Sarah saw a man in a blue cap standing under a tree at the edge of the park.

"Look!" she cried, pointing. "There's a man selling balloons."

As the children ran towards him, the man called: "Balloons! Big ones, small ones. Choose your own colours!"

"I'd like a purple one please," said Sarah.

The Rabbit and the Butterfly

Roger the Rabbit was snoozing on a mound of earth. Flowers grew nearby, giving off delicious scents. It was nice and warm. Roger could feel his nose twitching and it made him open one eye.

"Ooh! Oh! What's that!?" he cried, blinking.

A butterfly had landed right on the end of Roger's nose!

"Hello Flutterby," said Roger.

"Hello Rabbit," said the butterfly. "But why do you call me a Flutterby?"

"Sorry Butterfly," said Roger the Rabbit. "I didn't mean to be rude. But I often see you fluttering by. And you don't *look* like a fly. And I've never seen you eat butter. So that's why I called you a Flutterby."

Lily Lake

Baby Beaver and Betsy Beaver were walking home along the banks of Lily Lake; when suddenly the sun came out.

"Gosh!" said Betsy Beaver. "That sunshine is so nice and warm. And look Baby Beaver, see how it makes the water of Lily Lake shine like silver."

"It's beautiful!" chirped Baby Beaver. "But why is it called Lily Lake?"

"Because of the water lilies," replied Betsy Beaver. "Come along and I'll show you."

Betsy sat little Baby Beaver on a log and paddled out into the water until they reached the water lilies.

"Water lilies are really beautiful," chirped Baby Beaver, as he swam in the water. "I think Lily Lake is my favourite place!"

The Dragon

Sir Roger lived in a castle near the Snowy Mountains. It was very lonely there and also very cold.

One day Sir Roger heard that a fierce fire-breathing dragon had moved into a cave in the Snowy Mountains. So Sir Roger put on his helmet, picked up his sword and went out to fight the dragon.

The fire-breathing dragon, whose name was Dumpty, was eating some grass when Sir Roger found him. When Dumpty the dragon saw Sir Roger with his sword he burst into tears. "Why does everyone hate dragons?" he cried. "I'm a peaceful, friendly dragon. And I've never hurt anyone in my life."

When Sir Roger heard this, he invited the dragon back to his castle. And as Dumpty was a fire-breathing dragon, Sir Roger gave him the job of lighting all the fires in the castle!

Sad Suzy

Suzy was feeling so sad. She woke up feeling sad, and even after breakfast she *still* felt sad.

So Suzy combed her fur and tied her best ribbon on her head and went out into the fresh air.

As soon as she saw the pretty flowers she felt just a *little* better.

"I'm not as sad as I was before," she said to herself. "But I'm still not really happy."

Just then two tiny bluebirds passed by. They saw Suzy looking glum, so they flew down beside her.

"We'll cheer you up," chirped one of the bluebirds. "We'll sing a duet for you."

"Yes please. I'd like that," said Suzy. "And I'm sure that *will* cheer me up!"

In a Balloon

"Gosh!" said Mole, climbing into the balloon basket. "This should be a great adventure. Now where did I put my parachute?"

"You won't need a parachute," sighed Rat. "And you won't need those flying goggles either. We're only going up to tree top height."

"But I might fall out!" cried Mole. "I might fall out and land on my head!"

"You won't fall out," said Rat. "My balloon is very safe."

Suddenly, Mole looked down at the ground. "Help!" he cried. "We must be a long way up. Those animals look as small as ants down there."

"They *are* ants," said Rat. "We haven't even taken off yet!"

Sun Bird

All the animals who knew Betty Bird loved her. All the flowers and the trees loved her. Even the toadstools loved her.

Every morning as the sun rose Betty Bird would sing her beautiful song. It was so beautiful that the rabbits would run from their tunnels into the open air just to hear Betty sing.

Betty loved the sun because it filled her world with light. So she sang. And Betty's song gave her friends much happiness.

A little bear from a nearby wood heard all about Betty's song. Each day he would travel over to hear her sing.

"Well!" he declared. "Betty's song is sweeter than the sweetest honey."

One morning the rabbits were delighted to see the little bear raise his hat to Betty Bird. He'd brought her a present too. A box of sunflower seeds.

Sidney Squirrel

Sidney Squirrel was having the time of his life! He was so full of energy he chose the tallest oak tree to climb. After scampering up the trunk he leapt from branch to branch — right to the top of the tree!

Then Sidney saw an acorn right at the end of the branch he was sitting on. It was the biggest acorn he'd ever seen in his life.

At that very moment the acorn dropped. Sidney Squirrel watched it go whizzing down to the ground. Then he scampered down after it.

"I've got a nice idea," beamed Sidney, picking up the acorn. "I'll go over and see Simon Squirrel in Tree Top Wood, and give this acorn to *him*."

The Happy Duck

Farmyard Duck was happy.

"Quack!" She was looking forward to a quick paddle in her favourite pond in Duckland. So off she went through the farmyard gates, leaving the cows to 'moo' and the king of the hens to 'cock-a-doodle-doo'.

Farmyard Duck went waddling through the grass where daisies grew like stars. Past a big oak tree with spring-time leaves.

"Quack!" Farmyard Duck could smell her favourite pond ahead. Only another short waddle and SPLASH! into the pond!

What would make her day complete, she thought, as she paddled around would be if someone brought bread to feed her. "Two slices please, but no cream quackers!"

Leap Frog

Wendy and John and their dog Pip were playing with a hoop. As the hoop rolled through the park, Wendy, John and Pip chased after it. They ran down a path which led through the trees.

After a while they came to a little playground where four boys were playing leap frog.

Wendy and John stopped their hoop and watched the boys enjoying themselves. Pip the dog watched too with his head on one side.

One boy would bend forward and the other three would leap over him like frogs. Then another boy would bend forward and the others would take their turn at leap frog.

Suddenly Pip the dog ran up to the boys.

"Look!" said Wendy. "Pip wants to play leap frog too!"

"But he won't be able to leap *that* high!" gasped John.

"Gruff!" barked Pip as he ran forward. And then he leap frogged — right over a clump of daisies!

The Ants Paradise

"I'll find myself a nice flower," thought Arthur Ant, "and I'll climb to the top and see what's going on up there."

So Arthur Ant walked on until he came to the base of a flower.

"Here goes!" said Arthur as he began to climb the stem of the flower.

It was a tall flower, and Arthur needed to rest on a leaf before he reached the top.

Up, up, he climbed, higher and higher, until he was above the tallest blade of grass.

Finally Arthur Ant climbed into the heart of a cup-shaped flower and stood gazing at the pool of rain which had collected there.

"I've always wanted a paddling pool!" laughed Arthur.

Three Little Chicks

Harriet Hen was the proudest hen in the farmyard. She was the mother of three lovely little chicks.

"When my three little chickens grow up," she said, "they'll be top of the class at chicken school. And when they grow up to be hens, they'll be good hens, just like their mum!"

Even before they went to school, the three little chicks knew that 'one and one makes two' and 'one and two makes three' and 'not to go with any strange foxes'.

"I want my three little chickens to be fit and strong little chickens," said Harriet Hen.

So every morning at sunrise, Harriet Hen took them out jogging!

A Fair Deal

Rob the Red Squirrel was sitting under a chestnut tree brushing his tail. The grass was soft, the sun was warm and there were fruit and nuts in the trees.

Rob was a very happy squirrel — until George the Grey Squirrel came rushing by.

"Oh dear!" muttered George the Grey Squirrel. "If only I could go to the fair."

"Why shouldn't you go to the fair?" asked Rob.

"Because I can't afford to buy a ticket," sighed George.

"Let me think a moment," said Rob the Red Squirrel, scratching his head.

At that very moment a chestnut fell off the tree above them.

"There's your answer!" cried Rob. "You can collect a mixture of nuts, put them in a barrow, and sell them for a penny each. I'll help you if you like."

"Great! Then I'll be able to buy a ticket!" cried George with delight.

"Two tickets please George!" laughed Rob. "Because I'd like to go to the fair with you!"

Sammy the Seal

Sammy was a performing seal who worked in a circus. He could jump through a hoop and balance on his nose.

One day at lunchtime when Sammy was playing with his coloured ball, his trainer brought him a bucket full of fresh fish.

"Thanks," said Sammy Seal.

"You're welcome," said his trainer.

Sammy looked at the bucket of fish and thought a moment . . .

Next minute he was balancing the bucket of fish on his tail and spinning the ball on his nose.

Gently Sammy Seal lowered the bucket and dropped the ball.

"How'd you like to do that as your new circus act?" asked his trainer.

"Great!" said Sammy, clapping his flippers together.

Pip's Magic Moment

Pip the terrier had been picked to play in the All Star's football team. It was his dream come true! Usually when Pip the terrier ran on to a football field the crowd laughed and the referee chased him off the pitch.

Of course dogs don't *usually* play football, but Pip was a special dog. When the special day came, Pip the terrier ran on to the field and the crowd cheered.

As soon as Pip got the ball he ran fast toward the goal, pushing the ball with his nose. When the goalkeeper came out to stop him, Pip ran between the goalkeeper's legs and scored a great goal.

When the game was over, Pip fell asleep in the dressing room and dreamed his magic moment all over again.

The Magic Candlestick

Bertie Bear had been reading all about 'Aladdin and the Magic Lamp'. All Aladdin had to do was polish his magic lamp and a genie would appear to carry out his commands.

"I wish I had a magic lamp too," said Bertie Bear.

Later that day when Bertie was playing in the garden he found an old brass candlestick in the shrubbery. "I'll borrow some of Mum's brass polish," he said. " and polish and polish the candlestick. You never know. It might be a *magic* candlestick!"

As Bertie polished the candlestick he was thinking to himself: "If a genie appears I'll ask for some honey cakes for tea."

At that moment his Mum came back from shopping and seeing Bertie polishing the candlestick said to herself: "My little Bertie's a good bear. I'll give him some of his favourite honey cakes for tea!"

Billy the Baker

Billy Rabbit was a baker. He made different kinds of cakes and bread and carried them around in a basket. He'd shout "Cakes for sale. Five pence each!"

One person who always bought a cake from Billy Rabbit was Mrs Tipple who lived at the top of a very tall house.

One day Mrs Tipple wasn't feeling very well and so she couldn't come down to buy her usual cake from Billy the Baker. So Mrs Tipple asked a songbird to go down and collect her cake from Billy.

Billy gave the songbird Mrs Tipple's cake and said: "Little songbird, if you come and see me when I've sold all my cakes, you can have all the crumbs you want from the bottom of my basket."

The Kind Robin

It was a very cold winter's day and the wind made all the grass shiver. A little robin was flying around looking for food to eat when he saw a caterpillar on a branch.

The caterpillar looked so cold and so sad that the robin took off his scarf and wrapped it around the caterpillar to keep it warm.

"Thank you very much!" said the caterpillar. "I've never felt so cold in all my life! But I feel much warmer now!"

"I'll find you a nice leaf to hide under now," said the robin. "And there you can sleep until summer comes with its warm sunshine."

The Sound of Music

Once upon a time, Harry Hippo decided he could sing. Of course he couldn't *really* sing. But no-one dared tell him.

Harry was so sure he could sing he called a few of his friends together for a sing-song.

Crocodile came. (He couldn't sing either.) Lion came. (He was Hippo's best friend.) Two Monkeys and two Tortoises came (but they turned up by chance).

Finally Crazy Crow with a stripey beak arrived.

"Right!" said Harry Hippo. "What shall we sing?"

"What about 'Three Blind Mice'?" suggested the Crocodile.

"I don't know that one," cawed Crazy Crow. "But as it's my birthday . . ."

"Happy Birthday to you," sang Harry Hippo and his friends.

"Oh! What a terrible noise!" thought Crazy Crow as he flapped away. "Harry Hippo really ought to take some singing lessons!"

Big Ideas

Two elephants called Big Bing and Big Ben were bored. "What shall we do?" moaned Big Bing. "I'm getting tired of eating doughnuts all day long."

"Let's try a bit of skate boarding in the local park," suggested Big Ben.

"I've tried it," groaned Big Bing. "They've put a sign up. 'No Elephants on Skateboards allowed in this Park'!"

"I've an idea!" said Big Ben. "Let's take a plane to India and see our cousins."

"But Elephants are banned on aircraft!" cried Big Bing.

"Yes. But we can go by *Jumbo* Jet," said Big Ben.

Mr and Mrs Chimp

"Let's do as the humans do," suggested Mrs Chimp. "Do you mean sit in front of the television all day?" asked Mr Chimp.

"No," said Mrs Chimp. "I mean let's have a nice cup of tea and some cakes."

"Okay," said Mr Chimp. "I'll try it this once."

Mr Chimp watched as Mrs Chimp put on her apron and laid the tea table. He continued to watch as Mrs Chimp toasted some muffins.

Then Mrs Chimp made a pot of tea and gave Mr Chimp a cup and saucer to hold in his hand.

"Put the cup on my head," said Mr Chimp. "I don't want to be mistaken for one of those humans."

The Tidy Circus

The circus fun was over for another day. All the performers and the animals had gone home to rest.

The lights in the big tent had been turned off and all was silence. Only Poppo the clown had stayed behind.

Poppo the clown didn't know what to do with himself. So he went for a walk around the circus, whistling a tune as he strolled along. "Dumty Dumty Dee Dum."

The trouble was, Poppo kept tripping over tin cans which people had thrown away.

"I don't mind tripping over when people are watching me," he said. "Because that makes them smile. But I'd rather not trip over when I'm walking by myself."

"I know!" said Poppo. "I'll sweep up all the tins cans and the rubbish and put it all in a sack. Then I won't trip over when I'm strolling along!"

When Poppo had finished, the whole circus was so clean and sparkling that it seemed to be smiling. And Poppo was smiling too!